An Animal Family

FOXES AND KITS

By Jose Ventana

Gareth Stevens Publishing

Foxes have lots of fur.

They like to live alone.

They like to eat fruit.

They also eat animals like fish.

They use their ears
to find food.
This is called hunting.

Foxes have babies in spring.

Baby foxes are called kits.

Red fox kits are
often brown.
Some are grey.

Their parents take care of them!

Words to Know

fruit

kits

red fox

Index